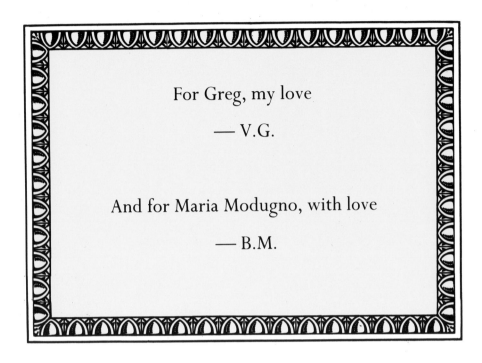

For Greg, my love

— V.G.

And for Maria Modugno, with love

— B.M.

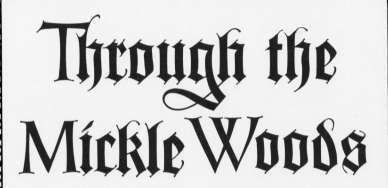

Through the Mickle Woods

by VALISKA GREGORY

Illustrated by BARRY MOSER

Little, Brown and Company

Boston Toronto London

Text copyright © 1992 by Valiska Gregory
Illustrations copyright © 1992 by Barry Moser

First Edition

Library of Congress Cataloging-in-Publication Data
Gregory, Valiska.
    Through the mickle woods/ by Valiska Gregory; illustrated by
Barry Moser. — 1st ed.
        p.   cm.
    Summary: After his wife's death a grieving king journeys to an old
bear's cave in the mickle woods, where he hears three stories that
help him go on living.
    ISBN 0-316-32779-4
    [1. Fairy tales. 2. Death — Fiction.] I. Moser, Barry, ill.
II. Title.
PZ8.G8535Th   1992
[E] — dc20   91-32882

            10 9 8 7 6 5 4 3 2 1
                        NIL

        Published simultaneously in Canada
        by Little, Brown & Company (Canada) Limited

                Printed in Italy

Through the Mickle Woods

T EVENTIDE THE KING SAT ON A
SOLITARY THRONE. WINTER SNOW DRUMMED ITS
FINGERS ON THE WINDOWS, AND ICICLES HUNG
LIKE DAGGERS FROM THE ROOF.

"I am weary," he said. He drew his cloak around him like a
crow folding black wings and closed his eyes.

The boy Michael stood before him holding a carved box.
"It is a gift," he said. There were bells on the boy's hat, but
since the death of the queen, he too wore black.

The king sighed. "It might help pass the time," he said.
And so it was the great king opened the box.

Inside, there was an opal ring, flecked blue as the boy's eyes,
and a letter sealed with wax. The king said not a word.

"It's the queen's ring," explained Michael. "She asked me to
give it to you when she was gone."

The king's hands trembled as he opened the letter. He read
the queen's words written plain as footsteps in the snow:

Do one thing more for me, my king, my love.
Into the dark and mickle woods go forth
to find the bear. This child will give him my ring,
and when the bells ring out at morningtide,
mark you, closely, how merrily they sing

The king stared at the letter a long time before speaking. "I will not make this journey," he said. "It is not fitting for a king in mourning."

"But she said it was important," said Michael. "I promised her."

The king's eyes glinted black. "Then we will go," he said finally, "but only because she wished it."

They walked in silence through the dark. Michael's eyes were bright, and he tried to catch a snowflake with his tongue. "Can you see?" he said. "My breath makes words in the air." He breathed out like a dragon and laughed.

"The way is hard," said the king. "You'd best save your breath."

"But it is so beautiful," said the boy. "The snow looks like sugar in the moonlight." He flapped his arms like a bird. "Watch me. See how my shadow flies?"

The king did not stop. "I have had enough of shadows," he said.

For hours the boy kept pace with the king, but increasingly he lagged behind. He stopped once to watch an owl, and another time he rested on the stump of a tree, but he did not complain.

The king watched as Michael struggled to catch up. "We will try to find a place to rest," he said.

They walked together through the cold until they saw a light, small as a firefly, from a cottage in the distance.

"Come in, come in," said the old woman at the cottage door. She hobbled to the fireside, her back bent like a shepherd's crook.

"Do you not know me?" said the king.

"I know you are a stranger who needs a bit of bread," she said, "and that's enough." She stirred the fire and yellow cinders danced like summer bees.

The king sat, rigid and dark, near the door. "I am used to the cold," he said.

"Suit yourself," said the old woman. She handed Michael a thick slice of buttered bread and plumped a quilt around his knees. "And will you stay the night?" she asked.

"We can rest only a little while," said the king. "We seek the old bear."

The woman wiped her hands on her apron. "They say," she said, "the bear is as fierce as he is wise."

Michael shivered.

"They say," said the woman, "the bear is as old as earth itself."

"Enough," said the king. "We must go."

As they left, the old woman wrapped a scarf around Michael's face. "Take care of this lad," she said to the king. "Keep him warm and safe." She stood in the doorway and watched them, until their distant shapes, like candles in the night, flickered and went out.

It was near midnight when they entered the mickle woods. The moon peeked through the black fingers of the trees, and Michael heard wolves howling in the distance.

"Stay close," said the king sharply. "I would not lose you too."

Michael looked up. "The queen said that to me once," he said. "It was after my mother and father died, and I was crying because I'd gotten lost in the castle."

The king did not respond.

"She told me I didn't have to be scared, because she would always take care of me," said the boy. He shivered in the cold wind. "I miss her," he said.

"I will not talk of this," said the king. "Come quickly now."

They walked together silently, and by midnight they arrived at the cave.

"We must wait here until we are called," said the king. He looked at Michael's questioning face. "My father brought me here," he explained, "to hear the old stories."

Michael moved closer to the king. "The queen used to tell me stories," he whispered, but the king turned his back as if the boy had not spoken.

It was not long before Michael heard the bear's voice. Deep, like the rumbling of mountains, the sound circled round him like a cloak.

"Come," said the bear from within, and slowly they entered the cave.

Michael saw the candles first, hundreds of candles that flickered brown shadows on the walls. And then he saw the bear himself, large and golden as a haystack, seated in a carved oak chair.

"My queen is dead," said the king, motioning the boy forward. "She asked that we bring you her ring."

The bear growled low, like the sighing of the wind. "It has been a long time since you came to me," he said. "Have you a question?"

"Why ask questions when there are no answers?" said the king. He turned as if to go, but the boy tugged on his arm.

"The stories," Michael whispered, "what about the stories?"

"We have done what the queen asked," said the king.

"But could we hear just one?"

"We have no need to stay longer," said the king.

The bear growled again, and this time Michael felt the ground tremble beneath his feet.

"You have more need than you know," said the bear. He drew them nearer to the fire. "Consider this," he said.

In a kingdom long ago there was a man who traveled from the farthest city to the nearest town. And as he went he traded things—a pair of shoes for a piece of gold, a parrot for a bolt of silver cloth—until he was more rich than he had ever dreamed possible. The people thought a man who had so many things must be wise, and no matter where he went they followed him, asking questions.

"Our baby cries," said one. "What should we do?"

"My father went to war. How will we live?" said another.

But though the traveling man could fetch goods from his sack and add up sums, he could not answer their questions.

One day he met an old woman who carried a wooden box. "Inside this box," she said, "are answers to all things."

The traveling man whistled. "I have seen many things," he said, "but I would give all I have to open that box."

"Done," said the old woman.

When the traveling man lifted the lid, he saw to his surprise that the box was filled with coins. Each one was stamped with a curious sentence. "Open the door," said one. "Give him your love," said another. "One hundred and five," said a third.

The traveling man was overjoyed. "I am rich beyond measure," he said. "I have answers to all things."

The old woman smiled. "But what good is an answer," she said, "without the right question?"

The king stared at the fire. "But this traveling man was not a king," he said. "He was not a man whose queen was dead."

"Whether we are born high or low," said the bear, "the same things come to us all."

Michael moved a little closer to the bear. "The queen used to say I asked more questions than there are flowers in the meadow."

The old bear drew him closer still, and Michael felt the warmth of his fur. "One day," said the boy, "I asked the queen why black-eyed Susans have only one eye, and she laughed. I liked it when she laughed."

The king scowled. "Enough of this talk," he said. "I have given you the queen's ring as she asked, and we shall not stay longer."

This time the bear's growl shook the walls of the cave and made the candles flutter like moths. "Consider this," he said.

In a kingdom long ago there was a man who lived alone. In spring he never sowed his seeds for fear there might be drought, and in fall he would not travel lest his ship be blown into the deep. But though he locked his doors inside and out, it did not bring him peace.

One day a bird, small and slight as a pebble, flew to his window. He marveled at her green wings and at the beauty of her song.

"I have heard that wind can uproot a tree from the ground," said the man. "Are you not afraid of wind?"

The bird cocked her head brightly. "Of course," she said.

"And I have heard that fire can sweep a forest in a day," the man said. "Are you not afraid of fire?"

"Yes," she said. Her wings, thin as pages in a book, glinted in the yellow sunlight.

"But if you are afraid," asked the man, "why do you fly? Why do you build your nest?"

The bird cracked a grain of millet in her beak. "There are things I would not miss," she said. "Every day there is morning, ripe as a peach." She trilled a score of grace-notes effortlessly. "And fledglings in the spring, of course—small things."

"I do not wish to hear of these," said the man. "What of wind and fire?"

The bird considered thoughtfully. "My song," she said finally, "requires them all." The man watched her fly away, as frail and strong as ashes dancing in the air.

Michael looked up and smiled at the bear. "And was the man always afraid?"

"He made his choice," said the bear, "as must we all."

The king moved closer to the fire. "It is not as easy as the bird suggests," he said.

"No," said the bear, "it is not easy."

Michael pulled his knees up to his chin. "The bird in the story reminded me of the queen. She loved to sing."

The king stared at Michael thoughtfully. When he finally spoke, his voice seemed crumbled, like the embers of the fire. "I cannot remember the sound of her voice," he whispered.

"It was like bells," said the boy. "Listen." He jingled the bells on the hat the queen had made him.

"I'd forgotten that," said the king.

"And her hands," said Michael, "do you remember how she used to make things?"

"She had small hands," said the king. He shuddered and for a moment could not speak. "I do not think I can bear to remember all of it," he said.

The bear growled low, his words bending round them like a lullaby. "Can you bear to remember less?" he asked. "Consider this:"

In a kingdom long ago there was a weaver who spun stories out of thread. One day an owl as white as winter perched in a nearby tree. "I should like my story to be woven out of clouds," said the owl.

"As you wish," said the weaver. The owl brought the woman strings of clouds as round as pearls, but every time she tried to weave them in and out, they would dissolve as quietly as dew upon the grass.

The owl blinked his great eyes. "Perhaps we should add some moonlight," he said, "the kind that shimmers on the water."

"As you wish," said the weaver. But though the owl brought baskets of jeweled moonbeams, worth more than the king's own crown, the story's cloth would not take shape.

"I do not understand," said the owl. "I have chosen beautiful things for the weaving of my story."

"Ah," said the woman. "But sometimes the cloth will pattern itself whether we will or no. You must bring everything, things chosen and things not."

The owl flew over mountains and through valleys. He gathered jade, green as ginkgo leaves, and raspberries, red as blood. He flew past peaceful villages and countries ravaged by war, and when he returned with all the things that he had found, the weaver smiled.

"These will do," she said. She took the things the owl had brought — threads of sunlight fine as silk and cobwebs gray as skulls — and wove them all together into a cloth. And when the owl pulled his story round him, it was so full of woe and gladness, so beautiful and strong, that when he stretched out his new-made wings, people thought he was an angel hovering in a breathless sky.

"So it was," said the bear, "and so it will forever be."

The king sat alone without saying a word. He turned to the boy, his face white as bones. Slowly and deliberately, he reached out his hand. "Do you remember," he said softly, "how she loved all things?"

Michael hesitated. Then, timid and brave as a sparrow, he climbed into the king's lap. "If I was sad," he said, "she would hold me."

"So she did," said the king.

He cradled Michael in his arms, as through the long night they slept, their dreams entwined like holly branches in a wreath. When morning came, they left the mickle woods.

They walked swiftly, stopping to rest only at the old woman's cottage. Michael laughed as they stomped snow from their feet and knocked on the door.

"We thank you for your kindness last night," said the king. Fluttering about like a gray dove, the old woman made them wait until she'd wrapped a loaf of bread for the journey home. Before they left, the king pressed three gold coins into her hand.

"It is small payment for bread so freely given," he said.

The king walked steadily as Michael ran ahead, then ran back, never seeming to tire.

"Look!" Michael said, and they watched the orange sun deftly escape the tangled web of branches above them.

When they were near enough to see the smoke from their own hearth, Michael stopped. "Listen," he said. "It's the morning bells!"

The king smiled. The snow, crisp and even as parchment, lay before them, and the bells rang out strong and clear. He reached down and took hold of Michael's small hand as if it were a gift of great price.

"Mark you," said the king, "how merrily they ring."

With thanks for support from the Indiana Arts Commission and the National Endowment for the Arts,
and from the Butler University Department of English and Writers' Studio

— V.G.

Paintings done in mixed media of ink, watercolor, and gouache
Color separations made by SFERA
Text set in Perpetua by Litho Composition Company, Inc., Boston, Massachusetts
Printed and bound in Italy by New Interlitho